COOL CATS

Exotics

by Domini Brown

BELLWETHER MEDIA • MINNEAPOLIS, MN

Note to Librarians, Teachers, and Parents:

Blastoff! Readers are carefully developed by literacy expert's and combine standards-based content with developmentally appropriate text.

Level 1 provides the most support through repetition of high-frequency words, light text, predictable sentence patterns, and strong visual support.

Level 2 offers early readers a bit more challenge through varied simple sentences, increased text load, and less repetition of high-frequency words.

Level 3 advances early-fluent readers toward fluency through increased text and concept load, less reliance on visuals, longer sentences, and more literary language.

Level 4 builds reading stamina by providing more text per page, increased use of punctuation, greater variation in sentence patterns, and increasingly challenging vocabulary.

Level 5 encourages children to move from "learning to read" to "reading to learn" by providing even more text, varied writing styles, and less familiar topics.

Whichever book is right for your reader, Blastoff! Readers are the perfect books to build confidence and encourage a love of reading that will last a lifetime!

This edition first published in 2016 by Bellwether Media, Inc.

No part of this publication may be reproduced in whole or in part without written permission of the publisher. For information regarding permission, write to Bellwether Media, Inc., Attention: Permissions Department, 5357 Penn Avenue South, Minneapolis, MN 55419.

Library of Congress Cataloging-in-Publication Data

Brown, Domini.
  Exotics / by Domini Brown.
     pages cm. – (Blastoff! Readers. Cool Cats)
  Audience: Ages 5-8.
  Audience: K to grade 3.
  Summary: "Relevant images match informative text in this introduction to exotics. Intended for students in kindergarten through third grade"– Provided by publisher.
  Includes bibliographical references and index.
  ISBN 978-1-62617-311-8 (hardcover : alk. paper)
  1. Exotic shorthair cat–Juvenile literature. I. Title.
  SF449.E93B76 2016
  636.8'2–dc23
                    2015029331

Printed in the United States of America, North Mankato, MN.

Table of Contents

Exotic cats have flat faces and little ears.

4

Their short-haired **coats** are **plush**.

The exotic is sometimes called the "lazy man's Persian."

This is because exotics look like Persian cats. But their shorter hair is easier to **groom**.

The **breed** began in the United States. People wanted short-haired cats with silver coloring like Persians.

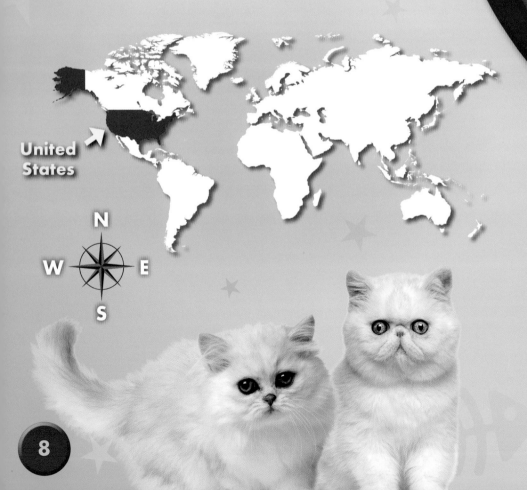

United States

N
W E
S

silver
Persian

In the 1950s, people **bred** Persians with short-haired cats.

The kittens had short coats.
But their **muzzles** were flat
like Persians!

They became a new breed. Today, exotics are loved family pets.

Exotic cats have **cobby** features. Their bodies are round and muscular. They have big bones and short legs.

Exotic Profile

— small ears

— flat muzzle

— short coat

— round body

Weight: 7 to 14 pounds (3 to 6 kilograms)

Life Span: 12 to 15 years

Their heads are large
and their ears are small.
Even full-grown exotics
look as cute as kittens!

Their round eyes can be blue,
green, or orange.

The plush coats of exotics are often **solid** black or gray.

Exotic Coats

solid

tabby

tortoiseshell

smoke

They also come in many patterns like **tabby** and **tortoiseshell**.

Exotics like to **lounge**. They often relax on tile or wood floors to stay cool.

They may get up to play with paper balls. Simple toys excite them.

Exotics are happy in homes with children and other pets. They are gentle and quiet.

These loving cats are always
ready to snuggle!

Index

The images in this book are reproduced through the courtesy of: ANCH, front cover, pp. 5, 14, 17 (top right); atiger, p. 4; Eric Isselee, pp. 6, 8 (left, right), 13, 17 (top left, bottom right); Taimako, p. 7; Trybex, p. 9; Juniors Bildarchiv/ Glow Images, p. 10; HTeam, p. 11; ArjaKo's, p. 12; Juniors/ SuperStock, p. 15; NaturePL/ SuperStock, p. 16; cynoclub, p. 17 (bottom left); Lukas Gojda, p. 18; Picsfive, p. 19 (top); CSP_vladstar/ Age Fotostock, p. 19 (bottom); Vytas Sinkevičius, p. 20; Alex Milan Tracy/ Sipa USA/ Newscom, p. 21.